Dear Parents:

Congratulations! Your child is taking the first steps on an exciting journey. The destination? Independent reading!

STEP INTO READING® will help your child get there. The program offers five steps to reading success. Each step includes fun stories and colorful art or photographs. In addition to original fiction and books with favorite characters, there are Step into Reading Non-Fiction Readers, Phonics Readers and Boxed Sets, Sticker Readers, and Comic Readers—a complete literacy program with something to interest every child.

Learning to Read, Step by Step!

Ready to Read Preschool–Kindergarten
• big type and easy words • rhyme and rhythm • picture clues
For children who know the alphabet and are eager to begin reading.

Reading with Help Preschool–Grade 1
• basic vocabulary • short sentences • simple stories
For children who recognize familiar words and sound out new words with help.

Reading on Your Own Grades 1–3
• engaging characters • easy-to-follow plots • popular topics
For children who are ready to read on their own.

Reading Paragraphs Grades 2–3
• challenging vocabulary • short paragraphs • exciting stories
For newly independent readers who read simple sentences with confidence.

Ready for Chapters Grades 2–4
• chapters • longer paragraphs • full-color art
For children who want to take the plunge into chapter books but still like colorful pictures.

STEP INTO READING® is designed to give every child a successful reading experience. The grade levels are only guides; children will progress through the steps at their own speed, developing confidence in their reading.

Remember, a lifetime love of reading starts with a single step!

Library of Congress Cataloging-in-Publication Data
Names: Ransom, Candice F., author. | Marlin, Lissy, illustrator. | Barrager, Brigette, illustrator. | Rosenthal, Amy Krouse.
Title: Uni and the perfect present : an Amy Krouse Rosenthal book /
written by Candice Ransom ; illustrations by Lissy Marlin ; pictures based on art by Brigette Barrager.
Description: New York : Random House, [2021] | Audience: Ages 4–6. | Audience: Grades K–1. | Summary: "Uni is generous, and plans to give Silky a special present for her birthday."—Provided by publisher.
Identifiers: LCCN 2020048613 | ISBN 978-0-593-37772-7 (trade paperback) | ISBN 978-0-593-37773-4 (library binding) | ISBN 978-0-593-37774-1 (ebook)
Subjects: CYAC: Unicorns—Fiction. | Gifts—Fiction. | Friendship—Fiction.
Classification: LCC PZ7.R1743 Uk 2021 | DDC [E]—dc23

Printed in the United States of America
10 9 8 7 6 5 4 3 2

UNI

Uni the
UNICORN

and the Perfect Present

an Amy Krouse Rosenthal book
pictures based on art by Brigette Barrager

Random House 🏠 New York

It is Silky's birthday!
Uni does not
have a present.

"I will find you
a special present,"
Uni says.

Uni and Silky
walk together.

Soon they come
to a field of flowers.
"How pretty!"
Silky says.

A mouse is there,
eating seeds.

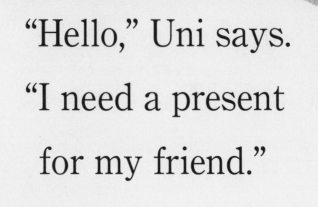

"Hello," Uni says.
"I need a present
for my friend."

"An acorn makes
a great present,"
says the mouse.

There are acorns
under a tree.

Uni gives one to Silky.

"This is not a
special present,"
Uni says.
"I like it," says Silky.
"Thank you."

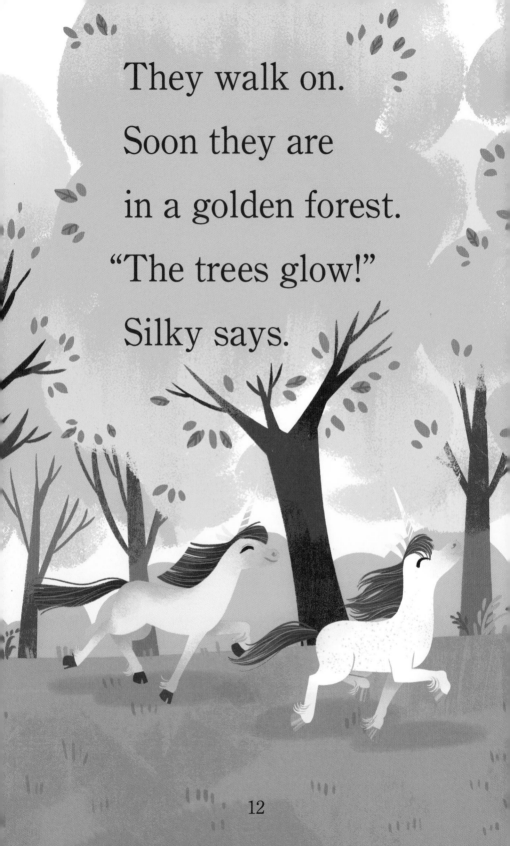

They walk on.
Soon they are
in a golden forest.
"The trees glow!"
Silky says.

A crow sits
on a branch.

"Hi," Uni says.
"I am looking
for a present
for my friend."

"A shiny pebble,"
the crow says.
"That is the
perfect present!"

Uni turns over some rocks.

There sits a tiny,

shiny pebble.

"It is just a pebble,"
Uni says.
"Look how it shines,"
says Silky.
"Thank you."

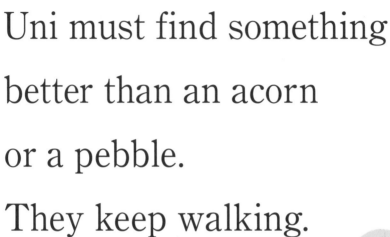

Uni must find something
better than an acorn
or a pebble.
They keep walking.

18

They see sparkly
blue water.
"What a beautiful stream!"
Silky says.

They meet a beaver.
She is building
her house.

"Hello," Uni says.
"What would be
a special present?"

"A stick,"
the beaver says.
"You cannot go wrong
with a strong stick."

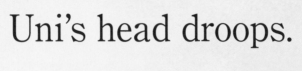

Uni's head droops.

A stick!

That is even worse

than the acorn

and the pebble!

But Uni finds
a stick for Silky.
"It is nice and strong,"
Silky says.
"Thank you."

Uni says sadly,
"I do not have
anything else
to give you."

"We had fun," Silky says.
"I wish this day
would last forever."

That gives Uni an idea!

At home,

Uni paints a picture.

It has Uni and Silky

with purple flowers,

golden trees,

and a blue stream.

Uni gives the present
to Silky.
"Happy birthday!"

"Thank you!"
says Silky.
"What a special day!"

"Best friends," says Uni.
"The most perfect present
of all!"